MW00830215

BRIDGE OVER SHALLOW WATER

WATER

A PWF SHORT WITH SNAP

MURKY MIDLIFE WATERS
BOOK ONE

JB LASSALLE

MIGHTY OAK
PUBLISHING SERVICES

CHAPTER 1

I was pretty sure if even one tire of my beat-up car crossed over the bridge before me, the entire thing would collapse adventure-movie style and send me plummeting to the swamp water below. In my mind, a dozen alligators snapped eager jaws, anxious to rip me to shreds.

My Jeep wasn't in great shape, a holdout from my college years that even my soon-to-be-ex-husband couldn't convince me to get rid of, but I trusted it more than this warped wood and rusty nails calling itself a bridge. A cobweb infested light flashed green from a signpost. The bridge was one lane wide, so the light was intended to keep cars from colliding in the center. I had to assume there was a light on the other side, and that it flashed red.

Yeah. There was no way.

I gripped the steering wheel until my knuckles turned white, the engine shuddering while it waited for me to decide. I held my breath, willing myself to move forward. But thoughts of how many ways this could go wrong invaded my brain.

How long does that light give cars to cross? When was the last time someone had checked the bulb? I peered through my cracked windshield at the faded sign attached to the light.

North Bridge to Treater's Way
Eight miles

Thick columns anchored the bridge, extending deep below the muddy brown surface of the Gulf, each marked with jagged water lines. These green, moldy badges of honor told a story about hurricanes past and changing waters. The air was thick with their mildewed stench.

A maniacal laugh escaped me. Worrying about a bridge's anchors, when I had none of my own, was the ultimate irony. These days, I felt as adrift and weathered as this dated piece of construction looked. Coming home to the site of my husband straddling his very naked secretary had shaken my foundation. I was weathering my own storm, and my water lines were way over my head.

So, who was I to judge based on appearance? For the last month, I'd hidden in my pop's house, ignoring the requests for interviews and faux-sympathetic clucks from false friends. I'd only taken my daughter's calls, grateful she was thriving in her college dorm and shielded from controversy. So far, no one had tracked down the mayor's daughter to ask about his affair.

My Aunt Ruth's postcard begging me to visit her in Treater's Way was the lifeline I didn't know I could grab. I retrieved the card and stared at the lovely landscape image of Bridge House, the family bed & breakfast I hadn't seen in over thirty years. It loomed larger-than-life atop the small island that marked the boundaries of Treater's Way, resting on the rocky shores of the bayou, a mansion somehow floating in the center of Louisiana.

Its tall columns and stately balconies were buried deep in my memories, as was my time living there. We would have taken this bridge, Pop and I, when we left Bridge House all those years ago. But the memory of it was lost in the haze I'd long associated with that day, and with my childhood. If it wasn't for Aunt Ruth reaching out, I would have forgotten it entirely.

I returned the card to my pocket and peered across the bridge.

Somewhat evenly spaced slats provided a road to drive on. I couldn't see what was underneath them, but according to the internet there would be a floor system. Maybe if it was called a road system, I would feel better. Allegedly, it supported cars, and allegedly no one had died on this bridge.

The barriers were a series of lovely arches, an intricate design that left me wondering how wood curved like that. It was barely taller than my chest, definitely shorter than my Jeep. It mirrored the arches underneath that curled over the shallow water like waves.

Arches were good. Arches meant support.

I shielded my eyes from the setting sun, shivering as a mild wind blew from behind me, as if nudging me forward. Crossing it would be bad enough. But crossing at night would be way worse. The tops of dense trees on the other side sent long shadows over the water. I really, really didn't want to meander through a forest in the dark.

And I needed to be away from New Orleans, even if just for the summer. I was a forty-seven-year-old empty nester who'd lost everything. On the other side of the bridge was a comfortable place to sleep and an aunt who, when I thought of her, filled me with warmth.

The engine croaked and roared as if willing me on. This was all I had. This Jeep and my two suitcases were the only things that were mine.

There was nowhere to go but forward.

I rolled down my window. If I crashed, at least I had a chance at getting out. I yanked on my seatbelt before inching forward. As my front tires crossed the threshold, clouds swarmed overhead and blocked out the last of the sunlight. A blast of thunder startled me into pressing my foot onto the gas, and the car and I roared onto the planks.

As if it agreed, the bridge groaned under the weight of my front tires. I held onto the shallow hope that, if this were an actual death trap, there would be a sign. Heavy bands of rain pelted my windshield. I flipped the wipers to their highest setting, ignoring the repetitive whine of dried-out blades. When was the last time I'd had those checked? Or the oil changed? Or the tires rotated?

This was a bad idea.

When I tried to roll my window back up, the knob broke off in my hand. The wipers halted in place, so I reached outside to wipe the window clear. Thick raindrops saturating me, I puttered toward the peak.

Either the car needed new shocks or the planks weren't designed to support a car's weight. I settled on the former as my boobs jiggled and my tailbone protested the not-at-all-light bounce of my butt against worn seat cushions, which now squished under me.

Darkness fell over me at the halfway point, but I didn't dare slow down for fear I would roll backwards. Besides, I wasn't sure the reverse gear worked, so I limped forward with my head angled out the window.

Even at the speed limit, the eight-mile drive across the bridge shouldn't have taken over twenty minutes. At the one-hour mark, the front tires crunched onto the rocky road on the opposite side, and I let loose breath I didn't realize I'd been holding.

As if nature was pranking me, the rain subsided and clouds parted, bathing me in dim moonlight. When my back tires landed on the road, my car let out a whine of defeat, and the engine died. My headlights flickered over the signal light—which flashed green —then went black, leaving me in darkness.

Cool.

I rested my chin on the steering wheel while water puddled at my feet. On the road ahead, a series of torch lights, each with an eerie yellow glow, lined both sides of a gravel road.

I was going to have to walk.

I flung open my car door, then screeched as it flung back towards me. A large body landed on my hood with a loud *smack*, rolled, and disappeared into a rustle of trees.

CHAPTER 2

I hopped out, cursing as another shadow pushed past me, my hip banging against the front grill as it stalked across the road.

"Don't you ever do anything like that again, you sonofabitch, do you hear me?" He hovered over another man, rocking on all fours.

The man lifted one hand. "Listen, I did what I needed—"

His words were cut short by a sharp kick to the ribs. He coughed and gasped for breath, curling his fists as he rolled to his feet. I rounded the car, peering over the shoulder of the huge man with his back to me to see his victim. A cut trickled blood down his olive-skinned cheek. Strands of golden hair were sweat-pressed against his forehead. He was broad-shouldered, muscle lining the folds of his ironed, button-down shirt. A dark stain along his stomach was the only thing that marred his businessman's attire. He dragged one wing-tipped shoe across fresh mud, like a horse ready to stampede. "Dimitri, your age alone does not give you ownership. You're not the automatic heir."

"I inherited the rights, Lucas," the man with his back to me snarled. "It's mine."

"Yet you haven't claimed it. Not properly." The man facing me, who I assumed was Lucas, took a menacing step forward. "You don't even want it. When I get the house, I can—"

His head snapped back as Dimitri struck him square in the jaw.

"Hey!" My feet charged forward without my brain connecting to the action, and I slapped my palm onto the similarly broad shoulder of the man with his back to me. "Hey, cut that out."

He swung on me. Instinct saving me from taking a fist to my chin, I staggered backwards, slamming against the hood. His eyes widened, and he charged forward. I curled my hands into puny fists. "Stay back!"

To his credit, he halted. "I'm sorry. I would never have swung if I knew ..." He let the words fade, anger replacing shock as he furrowed his brows. "What the hell are you doing crossing the bridge during a thunderstorm in this piece of shit?"

"It wasn't raining when I started over it." I rubbed at my throbbing hip, returning his glare to the best of my ability. I hated confrontation, and the intensity of his golden gaze was unnerving. He was taller than Lucas, with jet black, un-styled hair landing on his shoulders. His faded black t-shirt sat loose across his hips, but his chest was defined underneath it. His was a lean strength that struck me as somehow more menacing, even if he was smaller than the other guy. "And what the hell are you doing fighting at the foot of a bridge when a car could pass at any moment? You could have both been killed."

"Quite right. Common sense has found us, it would seem." Lucas strolled forward, one hand rubbing his jaw as the other extended. "Please forgive my very gruff brother. He would never hit a woman. I'm Lucas, this is Dimitri."

"I hope he wouldn't hit *anyone*." Despite the chill that settled across my spine, I shook his hand. It was creepy, how quickly he'd recovered, and his charm rang false. "Misty Ledoux. I'm Ruth Donergan's niece. She runs Bridge House." I pointed down the road, as if Bridge House wasn't the only building on this island. "She's expecting me."

I backed toward my front door as much to put space between myself and the two enormous men as to end the conversation. My car may be crap, but they would have to round it to get to me, and I could slide down the levee if I had to. Either way, distance felt safer than standing here with two angry dudes.

"Lovely to meet you, Misty." Lucas's voice dripped honey. A politician's voice, so like my future ex that it left a bitter taste in my mouth. I made a mental note to analyze that another time. When I was in a warm bed, perhaps. Or over wine. Not that I would think about this man and drinking wine. I mean, he was insanely attractive. A Greek god in the flesh. But still—

"... staying with Ruth?"

"Huh?" I swallowed hard. "Sorry, I lost my train of thought." And I was standing in near pitch black with built men who weren't afraid of physical violence. Why had I stepped into their altercation?

Lucas grinned, as if he knew where my thoughts traveled. Next to him, Dimitri's glare sent a shiver down my spine. If Lucas was a golden god, Dimitri was a dark prince. Not less sexy by any stretch of the imagination, but holy hell, was he dangerous. He oozed it, the way Lucas oozed charm, and I didn't trust either of them.

"... staying with Ruth?"

I blinked. Damnit, what was he saying? "I'm staying with Ruth. Yep." Flicking wet hair out of my eyes, I retrieved my suitcases and walked backwards toward the path, maintaining eye contact while giving them a wide berth.

"You're not driving?" Lucas pressed one arm across his brother's chest. Dimitri lifted his lips in a sneer, an actual sneer that sent shivers of menace down into my thighs. Or shivers of something, somewhere. I kept walking, my shoes squishing across uneven gravel.

"It died." My voice was little more than a squeak. "But don't help," I shouted, as if they'd offered. "I've got this." I stumbled backwards, using my suitcases as balance, until they faded into darkness. Then I turned and ran.

CHAPTER 3

*T*he beginnings of a blister nagged at my heel as I reached Bridge House. The brothers hadn't followed, that I could tell, and I had encountered nothing else to make my skin crawl during the two-mile trek. An errant bird called from a tree, and a vivid orange fox peered at me from underneath the bush.

But no muscular, angry men. I'd call that a win.

What was left of my breath escaped me once I'd cleared the forest and came upon the house. My suitcases slipped from my pruned fingertips as a sudden heaviness weighed down on my chest. This was not the house from Aunt Ruth's postcard. Not anymore.

Even under a night sky, the disrepair was obvious. Once lovely gray-washed bricks were layered with grime. Streaks of black ran down the sides, collecting at broken window frames. Rusted gutters hung loose from a gabled roof missing shingles. The towering chimney was a crumbled heap of bricks.

My throat clogged with unshed tears I didn't understand. I would have been less surprised to stumble upon an elderly man on his deathbed, withered and begging for water. An air of desperation clung to the land, and I couldn't quite shake the sensation that the house was reaching out for me.

Rather than walk straight to it, I angled toward the small parking area on my left, where red paint peaked out from the rusted fender of a mud-caked car. A memory flashed through me of a candy apple red Corvette convertible. A woman laughed behind the steering wheel. Before I could grasp it, the image danced away.

"Be like water." My finger traced waves through the dust on the windshield. For one long moment, I considered doubling-back and sprinting to my Jeep, hoping I could will it to life. The front door burst open, and a stick-thin woman with hair to her waist squealed from the porch.

"Misty! You made it!" She took the weathered steps two at a time, as if she were seven rather than seventy. The bottom stair was rotted clean through, but she dodged it without looking down and wrapped her bony arms around my waist while she giggled like a schoolgirl.

I couldn't bring Ruth's image to my mind until I saw her, but as she squeezed me close, I remembered her hugging me like this when I was half her height. The memory was the same. Sunshine and joy, hair that hadn't seen a brush in a hot minute, and the scent of jasmine flitting around us as if she were made of flowers.

I hugged her back, my fingertips digging into her soft green shirt. "Hey, Aunt Ruth. I've missed you." It came out before I could question it. This was my mother's sister, a lost connection I'd left behind when I moved to the city. I broke away to face her. "We should get inside. There was a storm over the water, and two men were fighting by the bridge."

Ruth dropped her head back in a cackle. "Those brothers, always at it, night and day. They're harmless." She stared down the road and clucked her tongue, grabbing my hand with a grin. "Don't you mind them. Let's get you settled."

They didn't seem harmless to me, but the journey was taking its toll. Despite the hot May air, I shivered. I followed her inside, where a stack of towels waited, as if she knew I'd been caught in a downpour. A hint of mildew permeated the walls, greeting me almost as fully as she had.

A small gust of wind followed me through the door, disturbing the thin coat of dust that coated yellowed sheets draped over the furniture. At least the cherry wood floors beneath my feet didn't creak, despite being over two hundred years old. This house had good bones.

Bridge House opened to a welcome parlor, with dual staircases leading to the second floor. Memories as faded as the paint on the walls took me up the stairs without walking them. Four bedrooms on the second floor, and two on the third, each with en suite bathrooms and balconies offering expansive views of the bay. My parent's room had been on the third floor.

"We don't go upstairs these days, though I'm sure you'll want to tour it in the morning. You can choose whichever room you want. The spare down here is ready for you tonight. Sam made the bed before he left for the day. Grumpy as he is, there's a soft spot for helping me with the physical. Why, just last week there was a lightbulb needed changing, and I..."

I let Aunt Ruth's words drift over me as we passed back underneath the staircases. On the far right was a massive open kitchen, which connected to a dining area and a large patio. I stopped to stare at it. The bed-and-breakfast itself had been closed for years. But two summers before I left, I'd had the idea to create a small cafe as a supplement. I'd been eager to take over the family business, even at ten, and make it my own. How had I forgotten that?

The name Sam rang a distant bell, associated with an aroma that parted the fog of my brain. Something nutty that smelled like home. We turned right under the staircase toward the kitchen. It was the only modernized room. A large, sleek looking refrigerator covered a third of the back wall. The overhead cabinetry had shining glass doors displaying brightly colored dishes and cups stacked haphazardly. It was a disarray of mismatched styles and shapes, as if the emptiest cabinet was opened and everything shoved inside when the dishwasher, an industrial sized stainless-steel number, was unloaded.

Next to it was a large gas stove with blackened burners. A small footstool rested nearby, and I saw myself standing on it, stirring a roux while a beefy man with a wiry red beard warned me not to take my eyes off it. *It'll burn if you even blink, girl.* I heard his voice as if he were standing next to me.

"Sam."

"Of course, dear. You remember Sam! He's run the cafe since you were knobby kneed. It's what keeps this place going."

In the center of the kitchen was a massive square island. On one side, water dripped from a farmhouse sink with bronzed fixtures. The opposite side held three peacock blue barstools.

"I made tea!" Aunt Ruth gestured toward a cup and saucer as if she were Vanna White and I'd solved the puzzle. Her grin was infectious, and my own broadened as I sat. I could already see myself having morning coffee here, overlooking the bustle of the cafe. Or enjoying a quiet Sunday with a good book at the window seat stuffed with cushions. The ambience put me in a dreamy state as the fatigue of the day blanketed me.

"I'm dripping on your floor." The words came out as more of a mumble than a sentence.

"It's your floor," I thought she replied. I sipped the tea, my eyes drooping while Aunt Ruth chattered, filling the space between us with stories from the past thirty-five years. I nodded, even as her voice drifted. "Let's get you to your room, dear one. It's such a joy to have you home."

"It's a joy to be back," I heard myself whisper, letting her drag me underneath the left staircase. Aunt Ruth's living area was in front of us, her bedroom door adjacent. It was closed, one of the few doors in Bridge House with a lock. The living area wasn't decorated to match the authentic nineteenth century decor like the rest of the house. Instead, it looked like a small apartment in a retirement community. Aunt Ruth kept jars of broken shells in a curio case. They surrounded a jewel-framed picture of her and her husband Stanley, like an ocean-themed shrine.

The room was small compared to the rest of the house, but cozy with a tv stand and an older model television set to Perry Mason with no sound. Her ripped, dirt brown recliner was draped with a forest green blanket, and a book was face down on the footrest.

"Thanks for waiting up for me."

"I don't mind waiting." She opened a small door to her right. I stepped inside. "I know this room."

"This is the room you slept in as a little fish. Rest well, Misty." She closed the door behind me with a soft click.

It was recently cleaned, or so the citrus scent hanging in the air would indicate. Not that I cared at the moment about anything other than being tired and wet. My eyes zeroed in on the four-poster bed across the room. My suitcases sat in the corner. I didn't remember anyone bringing them in. I trudged to the bathroom and stripped off my wet clothes, using another towel to dry my hair.

At the foot of the bed was a soft white tee and a pair of pajama shorts I didn't recognize, tie-dyed blue and pink. I slid them on and nestled into bed, asleep before my head hit the pillow.

The top of the Corvette was down, and wind roared through my ears as I braced my seatbelt from the backseat. My mother sped across North Bridge toward New Orleans. She flew down the highway. The wind whipped auburn locks around her face and large sunglasses covered her eyes. She lowered them to wink at me in the rearview mirror, pursing her red-painted lips to blow me a kiss as I wrapped my chubby little girl's arms around myself.

"You're not really cold, sunshine. You just think you are." She took a corner so fast I squealed in a blend of delight and terror. I tilted my face to the sun and smiled. The car screeched to a halt midway across the bridge. She hopped out, tossing her sunglasses

aside and pulling her dress overhead. "Be like water, little fish." She hummed a tune that haunted me with its familiarity and leaped off the bridge.

CHAPTER 4

$\mathcal{I}$ jolted awake to the sound of pounding rainfall outside, so intense and sudden it slammed against the windows. I stumbled out of bed, pee dancing my way to the tiny lavender bathroom.

Rubbing my eyes, I crossed the room to the bedroom and parted the heavy curtains. The back of the house faced east, and sunrise was not yet skirting the edges of the island. Despite the heavy rainfall, a rainbow arched low across the sky, collecting in a pool of color at South Bridge.

Except, it wasn't just a rainbow. Raindrops ran down it like a ramp. And it glittered, casting its own light against dawn. I pressed my nose to the pane and angled my head to get a better look. As I blinked, it flickered and disappeared.

As abruptly as it started, the rain died. The clouds cleared, and night lost its hold so fast I turned in my room to make sure I wasn't actually sacked out in bed, lost in a wild dream. The bedside clock flashed six, and my stomach grumbled.

After dragging a comb through my hair, I followed the loud clanging and a booming voice to the kitchen, where a man I assumed was Sam was engaged in a faceoff. His massive nostrils flared and his dyed hair spiked around his head like a lime green

I wandered onto the patio and backed against the side wall to take it in. The rain resumed, pounding on the overhang, creating a tinny song on the metal roof. Puddles collected along the edges of the wide flooring, but the twelve small dining tables were gathered toward the center and dry. Conversation was at a high roar to be heard over the weather.

Each of the wrought-iron tables was identical, though in various states of disrepair. Metal swirled along the bases, matching the high-backed chairs. Faded gray seat cushions adorned each, and though they were ragged and dated, the scene was inviting. Only two of the tables were unoccupied.

Worry piled itself onto the hunger in my stomach as I glanced at the window for a menu. The hours were printed in neat chalk handwriting—the cafeteria opened at 5 a.m. and closed at 2 p.m. —but there was no food list. If this was Aunt Ruth's only source of income, I had to wonder if it was enough.

I surveyed the patrons, most of them with half-full plates and bored or confused expressions, until my eyes landed on the far corner. A man sat solitarily at his round table, leaning with casual superiority against the railing. He wore a long black jacket that stopped above his wrists and a stovepipe hat. His beard dipped below his chin, and thin lips lifted into an unnerving smile as I caught his eye. I had to catch myself to keep my jaw from dropping.

I was staring at Abraham Lincoln.

CHAPTER 5

"It's not really him," a voice next to me whispered. The woman was taller than me by at least a foot, model perfect, with miles of jet-black hair piled into ringlets on top of her head. They framed her golden skin and accented the perfectly made-up face. She'd pulled off an amazing smoke eye and ruby red lips, made even more impressive by the early hour. A shimmering dress the color of Georgia peaches hugged her admirable curves. Even her strappy gold sandals reminded me of my honeymoon in Greece and the statues in the town centers.

I couldn't stop my fingers from tugging on the bottom of my shirt, which was wrinkled from a night of sleep. I only wore makeup when Daniel hosted events for fundraisers. On my own, I was a frumpy mess.

"What's that?" I angled to face her. There was something familiar about her eyes and the set of her chin. She grinned, showing me perfectly straight, white teeth.

"Walter over there. He's a Lincoln impersonator who took his job too seriously." She raised her voice at the end of the sentence, loud enough for Walter's knowing smile to downturn.

"Why isn't he wet?" A clash of thunder struck overhead. No one batted an eye or yelped in their seats, which told me I was

19

dealing with locals. Or at least people who'd been here long enough to understand the ferocity of a summer storm.

The strange woman cocked her head at me, her smile fading at my question. "Don't you remember?"

I blinked, shaking my head, unsure how to answer that question. The bored-looking waitress saved me. "You're over here." She twitched her head to the left, balancing coffee in one hand and plates across her forearm. Peering over me, she met the tall woman's eyes. "You joining her?"

A look of uncertainty passed across her face, and it was so out of place with her demeanor and dress I had the urge to smooth it. "Please join me. I'd love to have someone to chat with."

On the short walk to our table, I racked my brain, trying to place the woman behind me from the image nagging the edges of my mind. The waitress nipped over to another table to place their plates and cups before them, then placed a wide-brimmed coffee mug in front of me and, bless her, filled it to the edges. She set a plate of the same hash browns and breakfast tacos I'd seen in the kitchen in front of me as well.

At the door she stopped and regarded the woman who'd taken the seat opposite me, crossing one leg over the other, the dress's slit revealing muscled thighs and baby's butt smooth skin. When was the last time I'd shaved my legs? On a pretend scratch of my ankle, I ran my finger across them and shuddered at the stubby growth of hair. I'd let myself go the last few weeks while recovering. I suppose that was natural. No one would expect me to be polished all the time, but still. I could at least make sure there wasn't a jungle growing under my arms.

"You want anything, Iris?" The waitress called to her.

Iris waved a hand. "I've had enough coffee to fill my quota. Thanks, Kitty."

"Kitty." I lifted my mug with two hands and brought it to my mouth. The warm liquid hit my throat with the right amount of burn, leaving a bitter aftertaste. Chicory. I wanted to dance for joy. "She looks more like a fox."

Iris laughed, tucking a strand of hair behind her ear with long, painted fingernails. I watched her as I sipped, and she watched me without speaking, as if waiting for something to click. Finally, under the discomfort of silence, I blurted my name. "Misty."

"More like a steady rain." I made a gurgled noise in response. She was messing with me. She knew my name and thought I should know hers. But I didn't. I really didn't. So, I stared at her with my mouth open until she patted her chest and dropped her voice to sound like a caveman. "Me Iris."

The voice did it. The distance between the memory of her face and the memory of my youth closed. A warm wave of nostalgia washed over me. "Alex?"

"Iris." She leaned back, offering the slightest of nods. As I stared at the woman across from me, a flood of memories returned. Climbing the steep banks that led to the bay. Dipping our toes in the filthy water and giggling as crawfish snipped at them. Building castles out of mud and tiny shells. And swimming in the Olympic-sized pool for hours on end.

Before my mother left, and Pop took me away.

We'd hovered over our homeroom assignments, praying we'd be in the same class. And met on the playground every lunch and recess at Treater's Way elementary, the small school in town with the surprisingly adept educational program. My very best friend, who I'd sworn to write when we moved my last summer. And, somehow, forgotten.

A little boy named Alex.

I peered my head further and saw traces of my friend. The wide-set, almond-shaped eyes. The slightly slanted nose, a tad prominent. The way her eyebrows lifted when I was doing something awkward. Like staring at her.

I bumped the table as I rose, pulling Iris into a hug. Tears blurred my view of the rain as a connection I'd long pressed down re-emerged in the midmorning heat.

When we sat again, I used my small white napkin to wipe the spilled coffee from my plate. I blotted it away from the tacos, but the hash browns were soaked. Before I finished cleaning, Kitty appeared with a fresh plate, whisking mine away without another word. She was a damn good waitress.

The first genuine joy I'd felt in weeks engulfed me. I shoveled a large mouthful of the deliciously fried potatoes. "You look phenomenal," I told Iris, my words muffled by buttery goodness. She laughed, her shoulders sagging into what I thought was relief. I hadn't heard her order it, but Kitty returned with a cup of tea and placed it in front of her. "I wasn't sure how you'd react to seeing me. I was afraid you'd forgotten."

"Somehow, I did." I shook my head, as if a curtain was over my mind, and I was shaking it clear. I reached across the small table to squeeze her hand. "Pop kept me far from the island, and I honored his wishes until I went to college. And then ..."

I let my words fade. And then what? What had I become? A politician's wife. A mother. A caretaker when Daniel was diagnosed with cancer. Now, a future divorcee. "You stayed on the island?"

"I never considered leaving." She jabbed her thumb toward South Bridge. "I run a hair salon in Treater's Way."

"That's fantastic." I smiled, swiping at the tears hovering at the corners of my eyes. How had I forgotten this friend? It was like I had a wall in my brain, and some things were leaking through the cracks, but the rest was hidden behind brick and mortar.

Iris eyed me, sipping her tea while I ate, the clattering and clinking of tables and china around us fading into the background. As the rain subsided, some folks lingered over their food while others rose to leave. Walter, the Lincoln impersonator in the corner, remained where he was with his fingers steepled.

The cafe wouldn't jar any memories loose for me, but perhaps the island would. And I wanted to see how much damage the property held in the light of day. I was beginning to think Ruth had invited me here for more than a visit. There was no way the small cafe could support the house, especially if it was falling down around us.

"Want to walk around the property and catch up? I'd love to get the lay of the land again."

"We should do that! I bet Norbert will be happy to see you again."

I blinked, icy cold discomfort padding my skin, as the name brought a terrifying image forward. "Norbert is still alive?"

CHAPTER 6

*H*e was fatter than I remembered. His massive stomach sprawled so wide I didn't understand how his chubby arms and legs could move. His eyes twinkled as we approached, and I had the immediate sensation he recognized me. "Hey, Norby." Iris blew a kiss with one hand, her pretty sandals in the other while she lifted the edges of her dress to avoid mud. I'd changed into bright yellow rain boots I'd had to dig out of my suitcase, and as they sunk in the mud and sloshed through the wet grass, I felt more and more like a wobbly foal next to the glorious gazelle that was my childhood friend.

Norbert closed his eyes, as if he couldn't be bothered by us. With an effort that would make a man groan, he rotated his moss green body to face the water. His tail dragged through the mud, inching up and slapping down, dismissing us.

Iris chuckled. "He hates it when I call him that."

"It's good to see you again," I called out, glancing around to make sure no one heard me talking to a giant, old alligator. "My god he's the biggest gator I've ever seen. Still."

We strolled around the edges of the tiny island, giving me time to marvel at how little had changed. The rocky edges of the beach that led to the levee were still filled with shells and moss. It wasn't a pristine sandy beach, but it wasn't pure muck, either. A daring child, or a brave middle-aged woman, could scale the ten-foot slope to escape the house and lounge by the water with relative ease. The view of the bay feeding into the Gulf of Mexico I remembered clearly, like my memories reached the water but couldn't make it all the way inland. The shores were the same depth, as if erosion didn't happen to Bridge Island.

But the house showed its age. And, sadly, the neglect I'd caught hold of the night before was even more clear in the light of day. Bricks in need of a good pressure wash. Windows with chipped wood frames. Rusted balconies no one dared step foot on. It twisted my gut to see a house so magnificent it had once housed royalty in such a state of disrepair.

I shielded my eyes from the sun, now rising over the roof of the house, and sighed. "What happened to it?"

"After Ruth's husband died, no one maintained it. We've all helped as much as we could, but it needs a good caretaker." Iris's eyes burned into me, as strong as the sun heating my cheeks.

I turned away from the house, and we headed toward South Bridge. More sturdy than North Bridge, the mile-long footbridge led to more forest and the city of Treater's Way. Nestled at the base of the bridge, as if suspended between sand and water, was a yellow French-style cottage with a thatched roof. Bright pops of flowers bloomed in window beds. Forest green shutters added a homely touch.

"That's where I live."

The charm of it made me smile. "This bridge is well kept. Why isn't North Bridge? The one where actual cars drive?"

Iris snorted, her voice turning gruff. "That's a question for the Carpenter brothers."

"They're carpenters?"

"Not at all. They're filthy trolls is what they are." She hawked a wad of phlegm and spat it on the ground, wiping her mouth with the back of her hand. "Lucas and Dimitri. Disgusting creatures."

"I met them. Sort of." Granted, it had been dark and the circumstances of our meeting bizarre, but I would never describe them as disgusting.

"They're in charge of North Bridge," she continued, ignoring the confused look on my face. "Technically, Dimitri is. But he won't claim his responsibility. Lucas has his foot wedged to block any efforts to repair it."

"Why?" I rubbed my hands over my arms, remembering their violent fight from the night before. *You haven't claimed it,* Lucas had said, *not properly.* "It's hurting Bridge House. The only way to get to it is around, right?" At Iris's nod, bile rose in my throat. *Then when I get the house...* "What do they do?"

Iris folded her arms, lifting one nostril. "Dimitri is the town mechanic. Lucas is a manager at the bank, but he's got his sights set on something bigger." There was a flash in her eyes I recognized as betrayal.

"He's a politician." I rolled my shoulders to release the tension the word created. "I know his kind. I married his kind."

Iris clamped her mouth shut, working her lips. She cocked her head and lifted one eyebrow. "Where have you been for thirty-five years, Misty?"

I furrowed my brow. If there was a simple answer, I didn't know what it was. "In New Orleans. I met Dan at Tulane, got married, and raised a kid. And now ..." I let my voice trail. "I can't explain it, Iris, not really. It's like everything that happened before I moved away from here was locked in a mental vault."

Her expression softened, but the head tilt remained. I'd seen that head tilt before. I knew what was coming. Since word had leaked that Dan replaced me with his secretary, I'd seen that look a dozen times. Whenever I bumped into someone I knew at the grocery store. Or someone I didn't at the gas station. The head tilt preceded the clucked tongue or the word of sympathy.

It was why I'd taken to hiding at my pop's house. It was why the invitation to return to Bridge House had held such an appeal. But I didn't want false sympathy from Iris. I only planned to stay for the summer, but it felt good to think I might have a friend again. A real one. I braced myself, gnawing on my lip as I stared at the ground.

"I heard about your husband. Sounds like he was a real piece of work."

My head snapped up to catch Iris's eyes. There was a glint of mischief, and though the sympathy still underlined it, her words spread across me like a warm blanket. I laughed. "You don't know the half of it."

Iris draped one arm over my shoulders. "Let's walk, and you can tell me."

CHAPTER 7

$\mathcal{T}$he visit with Iris bolstered my spirits, but it also made me wonder what else I was missing. Somehow, I'd crossed that damn bridge and forgotten my childhood. It was natural for some memories to fade with time, but had I really become so involved in my life that I'd forgotten about dear friends and family? Precious memories had disappeared, and now that I knew they were buried, the shadow of them scratched at my subconscious.

I wandered upstairs to see what I could dig up, starting with my parents' bedroom. As I entered, a sense of barren longing washed over me. Mom had been a fan of shiny trinkets, all left behind when she'd left us, and they were strewn about in forgotten piles.

Most of the furniture was still here, as weathered as the rest of the house. Her reading chair sat in the corner, a faded white remnant of the times she'd curled her toes under and put a book in her lap, only to fall asleep gazing out the windows. The dainty pink vanity where she'd primp her hair and makeup was on the opposite end, with tarnished brass fixtures and a grime-coated mirror.

Between his offshore job and their fighting, Pop spent most

nights in one of the guest bedrooms. But my mother had loved it in here, and I could feel her presence everywhere I turned. I could see why. There was something mystical about the space, even now with the wallpaper peeling off, garish pink flowers wilting like they'd once been alive. This room had been like a grown-up version of a little girl's dream, and there were glimpses of my youth every place I turned.

Along the wall by the door was an armoire, cracked open to hint at the world inside. I rested my hand on it, closing my eyes to enjoy the texture of aged wood beneath my fingers, enjoying the vision of me tucked inside with a flashlight and a giggle, waiting as Uncle Stanley pretended he couldn't find me.

Her massive four-poster bed was in the center of the room, its weathered oak matching the armoire, but lacking the simple lines and curves it boasted. Carved seahorses, shells, and starfish danced along each poster. The sideboards' edges rippled like ocean waves. Mom had kept an ugly comforter atop it, with dainty flowers that matched the busy wallpaper in a way that gave me chills. When I was lonely, I'd creep inside and slide under the scratchy blanket, pulling it to my neck and burrowing into the scent of her.

Portions of the floor were warped and buckling. Everything tilted toward the balcony. If it were mine, I'd remove the wallpaper and sand the floors. I envisioned the walls now, with bolder colors that matched the sea, so resting in the room was like living in water.

Shaking my head at the fanciful notion, I scurried toward the French patio doors. I didn't dare step onto it, but I inched as close to it as I could manage.

If I woke up in this room, I'd prop my feet on the edge with a cup of coffee or maybe a computer in the early morning, when the sun would rise behind me and glisten against the bay, and plan out my day.

With a slight shift of my head, I could make out the shoreline and South Bridge. And if I peered forward, the tip of Norbert's tail pointed toward the water. I'd have to walk to the edge of the balcony to see him fully, but that would mean taking my life in my hands.

"You can feel her presence in here." I turned to see Aunt Ruth in the doorway, leaning against the jamb with a sweet smile on her face. Although it was the middle of summer, she was still dressed like a tree, with thick brown pants and a forest green turtleneck. I had to chuckle at her.

"Aunt Ruth, aren't you hot?" I walked over to her, putting my arm around her shoulders and guiding her further into the room. "The balcony isn't safe. We should string caution tape." She dipped her head to my shoulder. It was like I was holding onto a very dainty doll.

"It'll be made right again."

"How?"

"You're going to fix it." Aunt Ruth turned her face to me, her smile broadening. "I can see the doubt on you. But my Mighty Oak told me this morning things were going to work out the way they were meant to. She said you were supposed to be here, and everything would be fine if you listened to the house."

"The Mighty Oak in town?" I recalled a tree, larger than life, across South Bridge. And though the charming shopping center Illusion Square had sprouted around it some years back, I'd never visited, even though I'd gone to elementary school there. But why would Aunt Ruth think it could talk? Was she having a heat stroke?

Ruth winked and kissed my cheek. "I'm headed back after I change into something cooler. I'll be a willow today instead of a pine." She giggled, as if I understood the joke. "You and I can visit once you're settled."

She skittered out of the room before I could answer, and for a moment I wondered if she'd actually been there. A sense of dread filled me. She'd invited me here to repair a house I couldn't remember. I didn't have the skill set for that. Or much of anything these days.

But if the rooms were closed, and Ruth was spending her days talking to a tree, that left Sam to care for the café, and no one to care for Ruth. A nasty spear of guilt stabbed through me. I hadn't visited when my uncle died, nor had I checked on Ruth.

This was a family home, and no one was protecting it.

I latched onto the seam of torn wallpaper and lifted. It came off in a single tear, revealing dull ivory walls. For a moment, I toyed with the flaps. I was staying for a few months. I couldn't do much, but maybe if I cleaned the rooms, it would help Ruth get the place up and running. I could find a manager to care for the house. Gripping the paper, I pulled as hard as I could.

That old wallpaper was hideous. Fresh paint was all it needed to appeal to modern guests. Sure, the fireplace needed reconstruction, and the front porch was a death trap, but I could worry about that later. Or not at all. Removing wallpaper was easy. Tangible.

I kept tearing, stacking the strips on the ground, measuring my progress. I could find a hardware store in town and get the tools I needed. This room could be beautiful again. Easy peasy. I worked for hours until I lost track of time and every piece of wallpaper was gone. I'd balanced myself on the furniture, angling to reach the high corners. Dried glue stuck under my fingernails, and grime coated the nape of my neck.

"It's better already." I'd accomplished something. Dusting my hands, I splashed water over my face and dried it on my shirt in the en suite bathroom. "It's going to look great." I didn't know who I was talking to, but I felt like I was convincing the walls themselves this was a good choice.

I emerged from the bathroom and stopped short. Apparently, the house didn't agree.

Every strip of wallpaper was back on the walls.

CHAPTER 8

I fled down the stairs and out the front door, swiping sweat from my eyes. Was it a hallucination? A bizarre dream? I leaned against the railing, ignoring the way it shifted, and breathed in the heady air. I needed the earth scents from the forest to ground me. The musty smell of the Gulf soothed me.

What I got was a whiff of pungent gasoline.

I followed it to the parking lot where Dimitri Carpenter leaned next to my Jeep with his face fixed in a scowl. His black hair held gray at the temples. As I approached, round goldenrod eyes narrowed at me, making me feel like I was headed to the principal's office for smoking in the bathroom.

I met his glare dead-on. "Are you always scowling?"

He shook his head and crossed his arms, flexing developed muscles under his gray t-shirt. It fit in all the right places, and I wondered when I'd last had sex. When Dan was first diagnosed, we were like rabbits. Every time I turned around, his hands were on me, like he was grabbing onto something he would never feel again. But once treatment started, his drive faded.

Even years after remission, we never regained our passion. Of course, now I knew why. Still, my visceral reaction to this grumpy

His lips moved, though words didn't come right away. He shook his head, as if shaking me off. "Anyway, Ruth's always been good to me, and I'd like to help."

"Cool. Can you rebuild a balcony?"

He let out a sigh. "I'm not a carpenter."

"I mean, technically, yes, you are." I grinned at him, getting nothing in return but a bland stare. "Okay, so you can fix cars." I planted my butt against Bessie and crossed my arms again, staring out to where Norbert sunned on the rocks. What a strange day.

"Earth to Misty."

I tore my gaze from the levee. "Are we on a first name basis, Dimitri?"

He shrugged. "About the car. I want to be sure it works. The oil, shocks, brakes, etc." His own gaze drifted to the shore and his voice softened. "It's the least I can do."

There was something hidden underneath this sudden act of generosity, but the hint of softness in him was already fading behind his rough exterior. And I needed the car.

"Offer accepted. Thanks."

His fingers were calloused and his skin rough, but his grip was firm as he shook my hand. "Don't mention it."

He dropped my hand and strode away. In the spot next to Bessie was my mother's car, the old convertible. The waves I'd drawn with my finger uncovering faded paint. My mouth soured when I looked at it. On an impulse, I ran to catch up with him.

"Hey, wait. What about that?"

"It's a crime what's been done to such a beautiful car."

"Which is nothing, right?"

"It used to have a cover, at least. Blew away." We walked back toward the car, and he put a palm on the round of the hood. It was a seductive touch. I'd seen men do that with cars before. It was not something I understood.

From the opposite side, Iris approached. She carried a large basket in one hand and her hair was piled high on her head. She wore pastel pink capris and gold sandals with a cute little cropped top, reminding me I was still in the clothes I'd slept in. With a quick nudge of my hand, I checked to make sure I was wearing a bra. Phew. I waved at her and turned back to Dimitri.

"Do you want her?"

"Iris?" Dimitri shook his head. "We don't even like each other."

"No." I huffed out a laugh. "The car. I thought cars were girls."

He stared at me like smoke was coming out of my ears. "You want to give me this priceless convertible?"

"Not priceless right now, is it? Restoring it would take an act of god." He flinched, which I didn't understand, but his palm pressed tighter to the hood. "Look, it was my mom's car. And, you know, she's gone now. Not dead, but I don't need a reminder of her staring at me every day. And you seem like you could do something with it. So, if you want it, you can have it. As a thank you for fixing my Jeep, and so it's one less thing Ruth has to worry over. Or whatever reason makes you take it off my hands."

Dimitri stared toward North Bridge, ignoring Iris's disdainful sniff as she approached. He sneered in response. "I would like to keep an eye on things."

She lifted her lip in return. "Troll."

He snorted. "Hypocrite."

"Well." I slapped my palms together and rubbed them. "That's lovely, you two calling each other names like we are children and all, but it's been a long day and Iris has wine."

Dimitri did a half-nod. "I'll take the car." He smiled the first full, genuine smile I'd seen from him. It showed a hint of his white teeth. I suppressed a gulp. "Thank you."

"Thank you. Come get the keys in the morning." I extended my hand again, ignoring the way his thumb grazed my skin when he shook it.

Iris flicked her hands. "Be gone, troll."

I admired his backside as he trotted away. "Does he live by the bridge?"

"Log cabin underneath," Iris said.

"No wonder you call him troll."

Iris chuckled and lifted her basket. "Wanna have a picnic on the shore and get drunk?"

CHAPTER 9

$\mathcal{N}$orbert's jaws snapped over the marshmallow I'd tossed him with such force that I shuddered. Norbert may be friendly, old, and fat, but he was still a gator. And I was far too drunk to react if he decided I looked tastier than white fluff. I was pretty sure he was smiling at me.

"My mother used to go right up to him and kisshissnout." I took a swig from the not-at-all-small wine bottle wedged into the sand next to me and tossed another marshmallow at Norbert, then dipped my head back to marvel at the sky. This far from the city, there was no light pollution, and a dozen new stars created a canvas I wanted to drink in. The clarity of night brought new memories.

"I'd sneak upstairs and watch her from the window, here on the shore, wet from a morning swim. She'd crawl over and wrap her arms around Norbert and plant one on him." I puckered my lips together and let out a loud *smack*. "If I did that, he'd eat me."

"Norby? No way!" Iris was on her back next to me, hands propped behind her head. It gave me a false sense of confidence that, if Norbert did develop a taste for humans, he'd grab her feet before he got to me. She'd polished her bottle of wine off before the sun set but was still sober. Meanwhile, I was pretty sure there were three Norberts.

"He doesn't like it when you call him that."

"He'll get over it." Iris swiveled to face me, back facing the shore. And the gator. "Why did you give Dimitri that car?"

"My mother's car?" I brought the bottle to my lips, clunking it against my teeth and spilling wine down the sides of my mouth. I wiped it on my shoulder and continued drinking. "I don't know. It was an impulse." I shrugged. "I trusted my intuition. He brought my Jeep to me and would have fixed it for free. Pretty compassionate for a troll."

I squinted as the moon rose behind Iris, illuminating her like she was made of light. "You're very pretty."

"Sweetie, you're great and everything, but I like guys."

"Noooo." I gave the word extra syllables, letting my mouth hang open as I grabbed the rest of my sentence. "I can think you're pretty and not want to sleep with you. Your hair." I patted the top of my head, as if she wouldn't understand the word otherwise. "It reminds me of Charley's."

"That's your daughter?"

"Yep. She's working with the Mardi Gras Artists this summer. Designing floats for the parades." My arm thudded onto my lap. "She's gonna be a painter."

"That's awesome." Iris shifted until she sat next to me, swinging her manicured toes from side to side. "You must be very proud."

"She's amazing. And she has crazy curly hair like yours." I tossed another marshmallow to Norbert, too tired to lift the wine bottle to my mouth. Water lapped at the shore. A few night bugs skimmed the surface. "She would have loved spending her summers here."

I fiddled with the marshmallow in my hand, Norbert eyeing me with what I assumed was the gator version of *please, sir, may I have some more.* Summer humidity weighed on my shoulders. I rolled them to my ears to release the sudden tension building there. It was all so serene.

And familiar. Minus the wine. The near-full moon was blurred through my tears. "We used to do this all the time in the summer. Play out here until Pop or your momma screamed for us to come in." Iris rubbed at her knee. "I'd be all bit up from mosquitos and scratched from our traipses through the forest."

"You know"—I angled my head to her—"it's like I malfunctioned. After Pop took me away, everything I remembered about the island was foggy. I could grab pieces of it. I remembered Ruth, but no details." I craned my neck toward the house. "Brick and mortar." I turned back, running my hand across the ground. "Gator, sand, and shore."

Iris sniffed. "You forgot me."

Shame, ugly and dark, squeezed my chest. "I didn't mean to. And I didn't forget you completely. It was all buried in me. Pop said we would never come back, and he meant it. And I think I protected myself by pushing my emotions away. I wanted to come back, to visit you, but he said it was too painful. And I didn't want to hurt him anymore than Momma had already done. And then it all"—I wiggled my fingers in the air—"faded away."

"Do you always do what other people want to keep them happy?" Iris's sharp tone cut through me.

I lifted one shoulder and gazed out at the water. "I like to take care of people."

"Even if it's not what you want." Her voice was softer, and it took the edge off her words, but through my tipsy haze I caught the tremble.

There was more I needed to say. Amends I needed to make.

I opened my mouth and filled it with wine, swallowing hard against nerves. I didn't like confrontation, but I hated that I'd hurt someone even worse. Iris had accepted me back as if I had never left. She deserved an apology. I took a deep breath to prepare myself, then tapped her on the shoulder.

"Ow!" She rubbed where my clumsy fingers had jabbed her. "What the hell?"

"Sorry." I stifled a giggle. "I'm a little drunk. I was trying to get your attention."

"What?" She snapped the word out, tossing a marshmallow to Norbert.

"I'm sorry."

"I heard you," She waved a hand. "What do you want to say?"

"No, that's it." I hiccuped. "I'm sorry I left you. And even more sorry I didn't come back. It's easy to look at you now, after your transition, and think you are beautiful and brave and strong. But I bet it was hard. Even in Treater's Way, where people are pretty accepting. And I wasn't here to support you."

I dropped my eyes to the sand, tapping on the wine. "I can blame my mom and pop for taking me away. But I can't blame them for me not returning. The longer I stayed away, the harder it became to come back. And the fuzzier it got, the less I wanted to probe."

I gestured toward the house, with all its broken wood planks and faded paint. "The island is dying. I think I caused it." As the moon pulled overhead, identical streams ran down our cheeks. "You were my best friend. I never should have left you."

Fairy lights I hadn't seen the night before twinkled across the Bridge House. They glowed brighter as my heart lifted from the weight of my confession. Iris wrapped her arms around me, and we hugged it out.

"Well, that was sweet." I stared hard into my wine bottle, then straight at the ancient, large alligator who spent his days sunning on the rocks and his evenings who knew where. His long mouth opened. "It's about damn time you came home."

CHAPTER 10

A hysterical giggle escaped me. Norbert's mouth had moved. He'd formed words out of the side of it, with his jaw opening and closing like he was snapping. I swirled the wine bottle. "Is something in here?"

Iris shook her head. "She wasn't ready, Norby."

"Stop calling me that," the alligator said.

"You know"—I rolled to one side and stumbled to my feet, as if this was all normal—"I always thought Norbert was a strange name for a Cajun alligator."

"You think I should be a Boudreaux, perhaps? Or Thibodeaux?"

"Sure." I lifted the wine in his direction. "Or, you know, something less stereotypical but more French-Canadian, like Dane or Louie."

"Your family assumed I was Cajun. What if I'm from Florida, huh? There are Cuban gators, you know."

"Are there?" I held the bottle up to the rising moon to assess how full it was. "Maybe I should stop drinking. This is cheap wine."

"The hell it is." Iris snatched it from my hand. "I paid twenty bucks for these bottles."

43

"But it made me hallucinate an alligator talking."

"It did nothing of the sort." Norbert shifted his massive body, his long tail pressing against the rocks to give his fat stomach leverage as he turned to face me. "I'll have you know I had many a conversation with your mother in my day, and *she* spoke freely to me. Without the aid of an alcoholic beverage."

Whether it was the wine or the mention of my mother, I couldn't say, but I suddenly found the situation hilarious. I crossed my legs and plopped my butt onto the sand. I laughed until I sounded like a braying donkey. I laughed until I couldn't breathe and thought I might pee my pants. I laughed until I was empty, the house's fairy lights twinkling as if it laughed with me. Or at me.

"Too soon, Norbert." Iris shook her head, propping me up with one hand. "I'm getting her to bed."

I waved goodbye. "Night, Norby."

"Make sure you put a glass of water by your bedside," Norbert called out.

I stumbled toward the house with Iris's help, fits of giggles escaping like bubbles popping. "I think I'm going crazy."

"Uh-huh." Iris kept her head down, dragging me toward the door. "Get some rest. I'm sure everything will be normal tomorrow."

"I got this." I pushed her away and stumbled to the door. As I flung it open, I fell forward and landed on my knees. Using the table next to me as leverage, I pulled myself to my feet, extending my arms for balance.

Shuffling one foot in front of the other, I found my way to my bedroom and crawled into bed. The walls pulsed on each side of me, and the ceiling lowered over me. But it wasn't claustrophobic. It was a warm hug.

Head spinning, I wrapped my arms around the air. "We're gonna fix you."

CHAPTER 11

*W*ater.

Never in my life had I wanted water so badly. I felt like there wasn't a drop of it left in my body, as if spending the evening on the shoreline drinking had drained it from me. Waking up was like crawling out of a very long, dark tunnel. I rubbed chapped palms against my eyes, clearing gunk until the curtained haze of daytime flooded my sight.

This was gonna be a bitch of a hangover.

My lips were cracked, and my tongue parched. My attempt to swallow resulted in a ragged, hard lump in my throat. I stretched, pulling my arms overhead and extending my toes. But my legs were fused together, and my fingers barely separated.

And boy oh boy, did I want water. Norbert told me this would happen. *Make sure you put a glass of water by your bedside.* I'd waved him off. But now I needed a bucket of it.

Norbert told me.

I chuckled, the sound of it heavy and warped. I'd drunk so much I'd hallucinated a conversation with an older than dirt alligator. Dan had always said I couldn't hold my wine, but this was a new one. Despite all that, I wore a smile.

I'd broken through a barrier with Iris last night and paved a

45

rocky road back to our friendship. I couldn't remember the last time I'd had a female friend, someone I trusted who was there for me and not because my husband had money and power.

I'd messed up keeping her out of my life, and owning up to it removed some of the dark clouds swirling around my heart when I thought about Bridge House. And I owed more than Iris an apology. Aunt Ruth had loved me like I was her own, and I'd disappeared.

I'd abandoned her, and Sam, and the house. Even Norbert. And though leaving hadn't been my choice, when I had the choice to return, I didn't. Not only that, but I'd also blocked them from my memory.

But they'd welcomed me back with open arms and warm smiles.

I knew how being abandoned felt. And I hadn't realized until last night how much I hated myself for doing it to others. Me, forever the people pleaser, letting people I loved down. Talk about irony.

I'd made things right with Iris. Or started to. Maybe, just maybe, I could also crack through Dimitri's grumpy shell. Two friends. Family who accepted me. It might be time to consider staying longer than the summer.

But first, I needed water like I needed air, and lying in bed would not bring it to me. So, I rolled to the side, swinging my legs off the mattress like I was hefting bricks out of a wagon. I arched my back, my eyes still blurry, and slid onto my feet.

My toes wiggled like feathers, my knees slammed with a jolt, my nose smacked a floorboard. Stars danced around me like I was a cartoon character who'd been hit by a mallet. Shaking my head and batting my eyes until my vision cleared, I propped myself up onto my fingers, and my mouth dropped open as a gasp squeaked out of me.

Tiny, web like skin spread between each of them. I lifted one hand to touch it to the other, gently flicking the webbing. It tickled. Rolling to one side, I held both hands in front of my face.

They were my hands. When I wiggled a finger, it moved. When I stretched them apart, the shimmering skin strained. Holy cannoli. I had webbed fingers! A tapping on the floor drew my attention. I followed the sound down my legs to where my feet were lifting and thumping back to the wood.

But I didn't have feet.

I had a fish tail. A shiny, wide fish tail.

Fins and all.

CHAPTER 12

I'd never stopped to think what I would look like if I had a tail, but if I had, this is what I would picture. From my hips to mid-thigh was a deep royal blue. The hue graduated into a sky-colored aqua around my knees and toward my calves. By the time the color transitioned to my fins, it was a stunning blue-green. The tips were golden.

I did a little test, moving my feet from side to side. The fin swished. Bending my knees was like moving through tar. With strained muscles, I lifted it two inches. With a grunt, I dropped it back. I poked it with one of my fingers, gasping a little at the response, as if someone had poked one of my thighs.

I let my hand rest on it. It was smooth, almost buttery, with slight ripples that sent sensations of pleasure through me. And the sheen of it. The way my whole tail shined lit something inside me, like it was made of crushed pearls. I was a shiny, pretty mermaid, top to bottom!

At that thought, I clasped my hands to my breasts, patting them down. "Well, that's stupid, Misty. It's not like mermaids have shells for boobs. It's your bra." I cocked my head. My voice sounded deeper, with a gurgle. I grasped at my neck to check for gills, breathing a sigh of relief when I found none. How did mermaids breathe under water?

What if I wasn't a mermaid?! What if I was a Betta fish or a goldfish or something? The thought made my heart slam in my chest. With no evidence to the contrary, I was going to stick with mermaid until I knew otherwise.

But as wonder wore off, panic set in. The need for water wasn't a normal thirst. It was a longing deep in my soul. I needed water to survive, and if I didn't get to it right away, I would shrivel and die. At least, that's what I told myself.

The bathtub was the smartest place to go, unless I needed salt. Was the pool saltwater? Could I drag myself out of the house, across the front porch, down steps I barely trusted walking, and across the lawn without hurting myself? What did splinters feel like on a fish's tail? And who would see me on the way there?

My thoughts were frantic, my emotions flitting around like a hummingbird. Water would solve it. I needed to get to the water. I took a few steadying breaths, reminding myself to focus on one thing at a time. I wracked my brain for tools to help me relax. Would any of them apply to finding out you're a mermaid?

What if I lived in water forever now? What if I never saw my daughter again?

Panic was shoved to the side by blind fear. I flipped myself over and shook the end table, rocking it until my phone landed beside me. I fumbled with it, my webbed fingers struggling to hold it, then scooted closer with a wormlike wiggle until I was leaning over the screen. My shoulder banged the edge of the table, and the rest of the contents landed on my head in quick succession.

Lip balm. Hormone replacement therapy medications. A garish pair of reading glasses. Then, with a topple and a thud, a tall glass of water plonked onto the back of my head. Its icy contents drenched my hair and ran into my eyes. I wailed like a banshee.

Heavy footsteps thudded across the floors and the door swung open. Dimitri scowled at me, mouth wide open. He panted as if he'd run from a mile away.

"What in the hell is going on in here? Are you okay?"

"Uhm." It was all I could muster as I pictured myself from his perspective. I was soaked from the shoulders up, my body twisted on the ground. Oh yeah, and I had a mermaid tail.

But my vision was clearing, and I couldn't register shock on his face. He'd closed his mouth and pressed his lips thin. If anything, he looked annoyed. "Why are you on the floor?"

"I fell out of bed." My voice was back to normal, and I had the distinct sensation of something curling into a ball and falling asleep inside me. I wiggled my toes. They separated. I rolled to my hands and knees, wiping drips from my eyes.

Dimitri grunted, his golden eyes flashing an emotion I didn't recognize. "You're not wearing pants."

Like I was moving in slow motion, I patted below my waist. My pretty, shiny tail had disappeared. In its place were my legs, hips, and thighs. And no underwear. I pulled at the edges of the tangled sheets to cover myself, plopping onto the bed with the grace of a walrus. "What are you doing here?"

"You said to pick up the keys in the morning."

Had I said that? Yesterday was a distant memory. I gathered the sheet closer as if it might erase what he'd seen. "They're in my pocket."

He lifted the side of his mouth, propping one arm on the door jamb. "You don't have pockets, sweetheart."

He wasn't leering, the gleam in Dimitri's eyes filled me with heat. Angry Dimitri terrified me. Grumpy Dimitri I could handle. This guy ...

I swallowed. "My pants pocket." I jerked my head to my right, where my faded mom jeans were draped over a reading chair. Dimitri didn't move. My cheeks were on fire, and my stomach was turning somersaults. "You can get them."

51

CHAPTER 13

*I*ris executed a perfect swan dive off the side of the deep end, while I dipped my toes in from the pool's edge. "I'm so glad the pool is intact."

Iris furrowed her brow at me. "There was never anything wrong with the pool."

I ran my hand through the water, feeling the salty smoothness of it. The temperature was perfect, the travertine deck cool under my palms, and none of the tiles had a spot of grime. "I assumed it fell into disrepair. Like everything else."

Iris gave me a look suggesting she knew something important. She went underwater, turned in a tight flip, and popped back up. "Do you remember how much time we spent here in the summer?"

I smiled at the memory. "I do. Your bathing suits weren't as cute back then."

"I didn't have this amazing hair either."

There was something about how her gaze was boring into mine. And she was talking in riddles. I hated it when people did that. I slid closer. Something kept me from getting all the way in the water. The setting sun faced us from the shallow end of the pool. I shielded my eyes and slid on my sunglasses, stretching upright to catch a glimpse of the levee. "You can't even see Norbert from here."

"No, but he's there. He's always there."

"I always wanted a pool. Dan thought they were a waste of money. Funny, because he had plenty of it and didn't mind spending it on stupid cars and his girlfriend." I put my hand to my mouth. "I didn't mean to sound so bitter."

"It's okay, you know? To be a little bitter." Iris propped herself up on the sundeck next to me. "Hell, I'd be revving for revenge."

"Sometimes I want that," I admitted. "Sometimes I want to tell my story to the press or slip his secrets to his opponents. But it wouldn't make me feel better. And it might hurt Charley."

Beyond the shoreline, bay water darkened toward shades of orange and red as the sun lowered. "What's weird is I don't miss him. Not even a little. I was lost when it happened. I'd spent so much time taking care of Charley and Dan that I didn't know what to do with myself. But since I got here, it's like my time with him was a million years ago."

Iris pressed her hands together and leaned into the water, pushing off from the edge. She flipped into a backstroke. Sweet fairy lights adorning the bushes and patio lit, creating a little fantasy world where the water shimmered and beckoned me in. I hummed a little tune, my legs tingling as soft waves caressed them. I hopped in and went under, sitting at the bottom of the pool until I couldn't hold my breath. My tail did not emerge.

Iris splashed me when I broke the surface. "Finally. I was beginning to think you'd sit on the edge forever."

"I'm not the most graceful person on land, but I competed on the swim team in college. Water was like breath to me." I pushed into an easy freestyle, lapping the pool until I was out of breath and my muscles ached then floated on my back and glared at the house.

I'd spent the day removing wallpaper, only to have it return each time I left the room. Between that, waking up a mermaid, and exposing myself to Dimitri, my nerves were frayed. The more time I spent in the water, the freer I felt. In the peace of dusk settling around us, the very air itself thinned. Anticipation rose in me, as if I was on the block about to dive into a race. A few frogs began their nightly chorus, and I summoned my bravery.

"Iris, can I ask you a question?" Iris didn't answer, so I flicked at the water with my fingers, took a deep breath, and blurted.

"Last night, after you and I drank wine on the shore, I dreamed we talked to Norbert. I passed out, and when I woke up this morning, it seemed real. When I tried to get out of bed because I needed a glass of water, I fell flat on my face because my legs were not legs but a tail. I was a mermaid. And I didn't know what to do and panicked until a glass of water fell on my head and I had human legs again."

Iris's eyes bored into me, so I dove into an underwater handstand, staying as long as I could before re-emerging. "It all sounds nuts. I don't even know where the glass of water came from."

Iris was silent, but her gaze remained on me. She chewed on her lip and nodded her head. "Do you remember anything like that happening when we were young?"

"I don't know." I shifted to stare at the sky, not yet dark enough for stars to shine, but the moon stared back at me. "So much is still hazy. It comes rushing back in waves. It's like I can't distinguish between memory and dream, fantasy and reality." I squeezed my eyes closed. "It's probably a nervous breakdown."

"Maybe." She slithered to the center of the pool like an eel and winked at me. As she dipped under water, the colors from her bathing suit rippled out like spilled paint, until the water itself was a rainbow. They swirled in a whirlpool around her. When she came up from the water, her hair was a brilliant gold that glimmered without light, and her skin became an array of shimmering hues.

I blinked and rubbed my eyes. No matter how many times I looked, the situation didn't change. "What the hell?"

"I'm not done." Iris's voice was fluid, as if the words she spoke were liquid gold. She twirled in a circle, hair flowing and flowing and flowing as she grew several feet taller. She lifted her palms to the sky and dropped her head back. A rainbow shot from her fingers, arching toward the sunset, in a vibrant spectrum of colors I'd never seen.

My heart pounded in my chest. My throat went dry. "So, I am a mermaid?"

Irish chuckled and shook her head, lowering her hands into the pool as the rainbow faded. "You might want to take that up with Ruth. Nothing here is what it seems, Misty. Not even the house."

As she moved closer, what I thought was illusion remained. She was still taller and golden and made of rainbows. "I don't know how to ask this, but what are you?"

Her smile brightened the sky. "I am Iris, goddess of rainbows, the messenger between the gods and Earth. I am the bridge that connects the mystical to the mundane."

Deep within me, a small voice sang, as if all she'd said rang true, and my inner self was calling to be released. "Were you always Iris? I mean, even when you were Alex?"

"When I was Alex, I had not yet embraced who I was. I knew I was different, and I knew about magic. But I didn't know who I was or what my role was. When I figured it out, I became this fantastic creature you see before you." She waved her fingers like they were jazz hands and transformed back to herself.

"I don't even know what to say." It wasn't a useful statement. "That was cool."

"Misty, you closed yourself off from the island. You used to see it. I know you don't remember, but you were the one who told me my name wasn't Alex. It's because of you, and the words you said to me, I could transition into myself." She squeezed my hand. "And I'm here to do the same for you."

"You're giving me way too much credit." My voice broke. "Why don't I remember any of it?"

"My theory?" Iris extended her hand to point toward North Bridge. "The bridge, when functional, works for the island. Staying on this side keeps the magic strong and you connected to it. Once you embrace yourself, you stay who you are, no matter what." She sighed and dropped her hand. "But your pop took you away before you could figure yourself out. And as North Bridge broke down, it became impossible for not just you, but most folks who cross the bridge, to find themselves."

That lodged in my throat, and I swallowed against it. Magic had always been around me, and the veil between my childhood memories and my present mind was lifting. If I kept probing, I could clear it and see what was on the other side. It was more than my mermaid's tail or a goddess best friend. It was more than a talking alligator and a mischievous house.

But my heart was heavy as I realized this was why Pop had made me promise not to return. Since I'd arrived, there'd been a call. A song in my heart, playing softly. Now, I heard it like a boom in my head. The water called me to dive in and embrace the mermaid and swim forever. Tears sprang to my eyes as I hauled myself out of the pool and reached for a towel. As I dried, the song receded.

"This was what my mother heard. And why Pop took me away." I swiped at the tears with the back of my hand as bitterness coated my tongue. "He was afraid I'd leave, too."

CHAPTER 14

$\mathcal{T}$he next morning, I packed a breakfast, filled a thermos full of coffee, and headed down toward the bay. It was time to talk to Norbert. Literally.

"Good morning, Norbert." He was already sitting on the rock, like he'd been there for an eternity. He eyed me but didn't speak.

As I settled nearby, a bright orange fox scampered out of the forest and along the shoreline. It paused and cocked its head, gazing at me with familiar eyes. It was then I noticed it had three tails. She scampered past Norbert, who shifted his snout in her direction.

"Don't eat her, please. I'm pretty sure she's my waitress." The fox paused, and I swear she smiled at me before rushing toward the house.

I opened my breakfast and set it in front of me. Tossing Norbert a marshmallow and some bacon. "Don't tell Aunt Ruth." I poured coffee into the thermos lid and took a sip. It was a peaceful early morning, with the water sending soft waves to lap near my toes. The heat was not yet unbearable, and I could drink coffee and not feel like I was going to break into a hot flash. There were no boats to disrupt the music of nature, and no sound of distant traffic.

"So, after our chat the other night, I woke up with a mermaid's tail. Then Iris showed me her true form." I stared at Norbert. He stared back saying nothing. I tossed him another marshmallow. "I still have a lot of question marks, but I've learned this island is magical, and Mom was a mermaid too. Did you know her?"

I waited, holding my breath, until the edges of his lips curved into a smile.

"I don't eat foxes. There's plenty of food in the water." A low growl rolled out of his throat. "Though I've always wanted to bite a human."

I blinked a few times, but his smile remained. "Wine or not, it still looks funny when you talk."

"Welcome home, Misty."

"Home." The word tasted sweeter than my coffee. "Did we used to have breakfast?"

"You don't remember?" I shook my head, and Norbert let out what might have been a sigh. "Damn bridge. When you cross, it makes you forget things. Unless you've really held onto them. You were too young."

"I was twelve. Most people would say that's not too young." I stretched my legs and propped myself back on my hands. "Maybe I wanted to forget."

Norbert shifted to the side, hauling his massive belly with a shuffle. "What do you remember?"

I closed my eyes, letting the sun warm my skin. "The last day I was here. Kind of. It's fuzzy."

"Tell me about it."

I scrunched my eyes a bit as I visualized pushing aside the curtain in my brain. I wanted all the memories, every last one of them, back. But for now, I grabbed onto a stray thread and held it tight. "It was the last day of school. And Pop looked so small."

To my ears, my voice sounded younger. Like I was twelve

again, excited about summer. I let myself lean into it, pulling the curtain wider.

"I woke up early and helped Sam with prep work until he shoved me off and told me to go be a kid. I ran out of the house to meet Alex at South Bridge, and we bolted to the other side to catch the school bus. I was so excited for summer."

"What did you do during the summer?"

What did we do? "Alex and I would snag leftover donuts or breakfast sandwiches from the cafe every morning. We'd come down here, getting as close to you as we dared. You were always on those rocks, basking in the sun. Alex—Iris—wondered where you went at night."

I crossed my legs and sat up, bouncing slightly. "We'd spend the afternoon along the shore, chatting about everything and nothing, admitting I had a crush on Stevie Newsom and Alex did, too, and giggling about how alike we were, even if he was a boy and I was a girl. I'd paint his toes with really bright colors I'd snatched from Mom's cabinet. They all had magical names like Sea Witch or Mystic Pearl. When they dried, we'd wiggle our toes in the bay water until the crawfish scurried away.

"My skin never burned in the summer, but Alex's golden tone would turn bronze and his thick, dark hair would reach his shoulders. We'd braid it into a pretty ponytail and strut in front of you. I always got the feeling you understood us."

Norbert chuckled. "I did."

"Mom told me she talked to you, and you talked back. But that day I couldn't remember the last time she'd been this close to the water. Or spoken to you. She'd started hiding on her bedroom balcony, staring across the water to where it twisted and continued into the Gulf.

"When the cafe closed at four, Alex and I would help clean up, and Sam would throw us a few dollars from the tip jar in gratitude. We didn't want it; in truth, it was fun wiping the tables and setting the place to rights. It had been my idea to start the cafe, as a way to bring in more business than the four bedrooms that made up the B&B. To give more people a chance here. The sense of ownership, the gratification of something I created helping Momma not worry about money, brought me joy. But the dollars bought ice cream, and that was good too."

I tossed Norbert another piece of bacon.

"All of that lay before me as I ran away from the bus and across the bridge. I came here to tell you it was finally summer.

"But you weren't on your rocks." I scratched at my jaw, surprised to find tears streaming. "Pop was. His shoulders were shaking. His head dropped low. And one of his massive hands was on the back of his bright red neck. I didn't speak. Couldn't, as a big lump landed in my throat the closer I got. I knew something was wrong. I sat next to him, letting the sultry breeze off the Gulf slap me in the face, the hem of my uniform scratching at my knees. I patted his leg, my small hand on his massive leg. But my great big Pop was small beside me.

"And he let tears fall because Pop was one hundred in everything he did. Work, love, laugh, eat. Pop did it all to one hundred. So, tears landed on his thick blond beard and soaked it, and he wiped at it with the back of his hand."

I paused, inching closer to Norbert, resting my hand on his neck.

"Pop said, 'Momma is gone, baby. She's not coming back. And neither are we.' I thought I was gonna throw up, but I swallowed it down. I swallowed my voice, too. I wanted to beg to stay, to convince him I could manage things without Momma. I could run the café, and Sam would cook, and all the people would still come. I wanted my summer with Alex and the freedom I only got when we swam."

My breath came out in a shudder. "But Daddy looked so small, and I was afraid anything I asked for in that moment would make him look smaller. I didn't ask for it. 'It's you and me now, kid,' he told me. And I agreed, staring out at the water, positive I'd never see it again."

Fat tears dropped from Norbert's eyes, and I nuzzled into his neck without thinking.

"And there you were. Swimming in a circle with the saddest expression I've ever seen on an alligator. I waved at you, and you dropped below the surface."

When he spoke again, his voice was gruff. "I loved your mother very much. She was a good friend." A glint of humor returned to his eyes. "So were you."

I squeezed him close and retreated to my blanket, dragging my fingers through the sand. "I kind of remember having breakfast here. Mom would jump in the water for a swim, but I would never go, because I thought the water was gross. And I figured just because *you* didn't eat me didn't mean some other gator wouldn't."

"Even the true gators would never eat a mermaid. That's rude."

My head snapped up. "You're not a true alligator?"

"I am a familiar."

"A what now?"

"I take the form of an animal and help magical beings. Most witches have them. Cats or bats." He winked at me, and waking up as a mermaid suddenly seemed like no big deal. "I chose a gator. I was your mother's familiar, and I was your grandmother's as well."

"Are you Ruth's familiar?" Did I need to make sure Norbert ate more than marshmallows and bacon?

"I've never officially been Ruth's. But she's always taken care of me like one. That's why she won't feed me bacon or marshmallows."

"So, you're my familiar."

"I will be, one day. When you're ready."

I let that digest. I had a pet alligator. Sort of. "This island is really weird, isn't it?"

"It sure is," Norbert replied. "That's one of my favorite things about it."

CHAPTER 15

I tapped my toe to an unnamed tune on the broken
floor beneath the porch swing I didn't quite trust to
hold my weight. It groaned if I shifted too far, and the wooden
slats needed refinishing. The swing itself repeated a warning creak
as I fidgeted.

The soft melody she always hummed reached me as she
neared the house. When she saw me, her smile broadened and her
eyes lit. "Did you know you used to sit there when you were a
little girl?"

I didn't have any memory of sitting on the porch when I was a
little girl, but I believed her. Hearing her say it, I knew it was true
because it sparked familiarity inside me. The surrounding wood
sighed, as if the house remembered, too.

"Long day in Illusion Square?"

She skipped up the stairs two at a time and plopped down
next to me on the swing. I grabbed the rusted chain-link in time
to keep us both from tipping forward.

Aunt Ruth giggled. "I had a pleasant chat with the Mighty
Oak today. It was so much fun I lost track of time."

There was a glint in her eyes, a hint of the wisdom and
knowledge hidden under her buoyant exterior. I was in awe of her

upbeat demeanor. When my mother left, Ruth had lost her sister. And since Pop took me across the bridge, she'd lost her niece that day, too. Now, her husband was gone, and the only home she ever knew was falling down around her.

But she still wore a smile. Of course, she also talked to trees. "What did the Oak have to say today?"

Aunt Ruth didn't answer. She folded her hands in her lap and waited as if she knew I had something to say. I fidgeted for a minute, staring at my twiddling fingers until my words flowed.

"Yesterday, I woke up with a mermaid tail. I think it had to do with too much wine the night before. But, I talked to Iris about it and discovered she's a rainbow goddess or something awesome like that. And I talked with Norbert. We had an actual conversation. So, what I want to know from you is ..."

Her face was as serene as when I'd started my word blurt. Her eyes were as sharp. "Am I a mermaid? Actually, that's not even the question I want to ask." I took her hands in mine because I needed the warmth of human contact. The reassurance of family. "Are you a mermaid, too?"

Ruth held my eyes for a few moments, her face placid. "Do you know why I like to see you sitting on the porch? It's not only because it's something you did when you were a little girl. It's because the porch says something. Do you want to know what it says?"

I braced myself for a ramble. "What does it say?"

"The porch says home. It's the place we welcome new guests and visitors, and we turn them into family. It's a place we convene. It's where we show the world who we are." She giggled to herself, then reached forward and patted the banister. "Isn't it funny that a few planks of wood and stairs could say so much?"

I swallowed the lump in my throat. "The porch matters because it's what we show to the outside world. But it's not always the same as what's inside, is it?"

I cringed as Aunt Ruth slid closer to me, vicariously feeling the sting of a hundred splinters on her butt. She dropped her head to my shoulder, and I put my arm around her. We let the porch swing creak as everything we hadn't yet said settled around us.

"Yes, honey, your mother and I were mermaids." She shifted to face me. Her eyes were full of wonder, wider and rounder than usual. "I abandoned my tail for Stanley. I heard the call of the sea, but the call of my heart was stronger. The song we hear is uniquely ours and guides us where we're meant to go. We thought your mother was meant for Bridge House, but she was headed to the water when she—"

"Met Pop," I finished for her. "She got pregnant with me. And tried to choose the call of her heart."

Ruth's lips trembled. "Someone from our family has cared for Bridge House as long as it's been around. It needs somebody who understands what it means to make choices. Someone who can help guests find their paths as well. For me, the choice was simple. As soon as I met Stanley, I knew. He was my home. I didn't need a tail. He never knew I had one!"

She turned her head to look out at the water. "When your mother got pregnant, she decided to stay and take care of Bridge House. Because the choice had been a struggle for her, she thought she could help others understand their struggles. But she never had to care for the house, or anyone in it. Not really." She turned again to face me. "Do you know why she never had to manage Bridge House?"

I understood the answer, even as more memories returned in vivid detail. Mom and me in the convertible, flying like the wind before screeching to a halt at North Bridge. She'd dive into the water, tail glistening in the sun while I peered over the rails, terrified to join her yet longing to at the same time.

I'd inch her car home, young as I was, and wait on the porch for her return. I'd tell the house I was terrified this would be the time she didn't come back. And, certain it understood, I developed a kinship with it. I'd pass the time by cleaning the rooms and tending to guests. I made plans for the cafe and hired a cook. Eager to please her, to give her the freedom to swim.

Because I loved the house. And hoped it would be enough to make her stay.

"She never had to help out with Bridge House because it belonged to me."

Ruth brushed her dry hands over mine, the sound of it rustling like paper. "You were always doing something to make the house better. Eventually, it didn't need her at all."

I'd needed her, though. And I'd been so desperate to keep her I'd taken away any purpose she might have had on land. Until, in my desire to make her stay, I'd made it easier for her to leave. I couldn't blame myself. I was too young to understand, but I had to wonder.

"Aunt Ruth, did she ever love me?"

Asking that question out loud—even at my age—brought the pain of my mom leaving to the surface. It was as if she had left yesterday rather than thirty-five years ago. I'd never tried to look for her. I never asked where she went. I'd known she didn't want to be with us, there was somewhere else she would rather be, and I'd been afraid that if I found her and asked if she loved me, I wouldn't get the answer I wanted.

Or maybe I would get the answer I feared.

And I'd spent my life seeking love, acceptance, and approval from every outside source I could find. Taking care of Bridge House morphed into taking care of Pop. Then I managed Dan's campaigns and cared for him when he got sick. And I got so lost in that I didn't realize he'd stopped caring about me. I'd become part of his image, a part that made him look good and held cocktail parties but never asked for anything for herself.

But it also led to Charley. Caring for her had never felt like a chore, and I hadn't done it because I needed her to love me. I'd done it because I loved my daughter. And as I looked back at my time at Bridge House, I realized I had loved the house, too.

Like a foundation repaired, the curtain cleared, and all my memories were solid again. I dug my fingers into the swing. Beside me, Aunt Ruth snored. She wouldn't answer my question, but I wasn't sure she knew the answer. That was okay. I didn't need my aunt to answer me. For the first time in my life, I needed to find that answer on my own.

And I was pretty sure I could find it on Bridge Island. Unless we lost the house. I nudged her awake. "Aunt Ruth, how bad are the finances?"

She shifted to face me, a wave of sadness creasing her brow. "Lucas says I have three months."

"Lucas Carpenter? Dimitri's brother?"

"He runs the bank in Treater's Way. He's been so helpful." She flounced backwards, sinking low. "I shouldn't have waited, but I thought you weren't ready. Now, I think I waited too long."

Somewhere off in the distance, something splashed into the water, disrupting the wave of cricket chirps. Frogs croaked their mating chorus from the small pond in the gardens. "Three months," I murmured, more to myself than to Aunt Ruth. "The pool is great, but the gardens are a mess. We'd have to fix the exterior and repair the fireplace. But maybe if we opened up one or two bedrooms ..."

I could picture the house in my mind, revitalized and flourishing. People would come and go, and I saw myself as the perfect hostess, greeting them, offering them breakfast coupons for the cafe. Aunt Ruth could live comfortably. The house would stay in the family. Become mine again. It tickled something I didn't recognize, ownership and pride I hadn't felt in years welling inside. Mine. Something for me to care for. People to serve and talk to.

Three months.

I let the weight on my heart release in a long breath. I'd once organized a charity gala for Dan's campaign on shorter notice. I'd fed and entertained five hundred people, selling it out within the span of a week. I could handle a house. I rose to the banister, running my hands along it, cursing as slivers of wood pierced my fingers.

"Aunt Ruth, tomorrow, I want you to take me to see Lucas Carpenter at the bank."

Ruth clapped her hands. "We can swing by Illusion Square so you can meet The Eight and my Mighty Oak!"

I didn't know what The Eight were, and I was slightly less excited than Aunt Ruth to meet a tree, but I clapped with her. A piece of the banister wobbled against my hip. I scrambled to avoid falling into the mud below.

There was landscaping to be done. And pictures for a new website ...

Hope and fear warred within. If I succeeded, I'd keep the island safe.

Of course, if I failed, the home where generations of my family lived would become bank property, and probably be auctioned off to some franchise then turned into a cookie cutter version of a New Orleans classic.

Or Lucas would take ownership and complete whatever plan he'd fought with his brother over. I could have sworn the patio shuddered beneath my feet.

"Okay, Aunt Ruth, one day at a time." I extended my hand, lifting her tiny body and draping my arm across her bony shoulders. "Let's get you to bed. Tomorrow, we hit the bank."

"And Illusion Square!"

"And Illusion Square." I squeezed her to me. She'd always been so childlike, so full of wonder, and it lightened my heart to see life hadn't ripped that away from her. "Do they have coffee in Illusion Square? Really good coffee?"

"They sure do." She rubbed her hand over her tummy. "And really good cookies."

"Well, that settles it." I closed the massive door behind us. The lock creaked as I wrenched it into place, as if it hadn't been used in years. "Tomorrow, I'm getting a cookie."

CHAPTER 16

"What a pleasant surprise to see you again, Mrs. Ledoux." Lucas Carpenter rose to greet us as we entered his glass-enclosed office, gesturing to the two chairs in front of his massive mahogany desk. "And under much nicer circumstances. Please have a seat."

He smoothed the front of his crisp button-down shirt and leaned back in his high-backed leather chair. His golden-blond hair had not a lock out of place, his square jaw was clean-shaven, and no trace of the cut from his fight with Dimitri marred his perfect face. He either healed fast or was skilled at wearing makeup.

"Nice to see you, too. Who knew we'd be running into each other again?"

His polite chuckle didn't reach his eyes as he steepled his fingers. "I must apologize again for my brother's behavior on the bridge. What you witnessed was out of character for us both."

Even though my insides screamed to get out of the room and scrub his aura off me, I squashed them down. Just like that night on the bridge, he rang false. Every movement was practiced. His smile was schooled even as he shuffled papers on his desk that I was fairly certain were blank, and a game of solitaire reflected off his computer screen onto the window behind him.

But he was the first step in getting Aunt Ruth out from underneath her debt and putting Bridge House back to rights. He may be smarmy as hell, but I'd dealt with worse. So, I dug deep and pulled out my best politician's wife voice. "I'm sure it was an unusual evening all around, Mr. Carpenter. I'm happy we get to meet again and restore our image of one another." I placed my hand in my lap, even as bitterness coated my tongue, and I longed for the sweetness of that cookie.

"Call me Lucas." He waved his hand, as if waving away the past.

He winked, actually winked, as his smile turned lascivious. I suppressed a snort. "Of course, Lucas. And you can call me Misty."

"Misty it is." He shifted his charm to my aunt. "Ruth, it's always a joy to have you in my office."

Ruth giggled like a schoolgirl. Oh, dear. "Hi, Lucas, thanks for seeing us today."

"Yes." He turned to his keyboard and tapped away at a few keys. Behind him, the solitaire game remained on display. "I have your account here. I must remind you both Misty is not an authorized party on your house lien. I'm only open to discussing this as a favor to you, Ruth. After all"—he leaned forward to prop his forearms on the desk—"you were a dear friend to my mother, particularly in her last few years."

Genuine sadness darkened his expression as Ruth reached out to pat his hand. "Thank you, dear."

"Yes, well, unfortunately, my generosity can only reach so far before I get into trouble with my boss. You're six months behind on your loan, and Bridge House is collateral I'd hate to see you lose."

"Lucas." I cleared my throat. "I'm a little surprised this loan went through at all, given that the B&B portion has been closed all these years. It seems there was never any real hope of recovering the loan. There's only so much money a cafe that's open with limited hours can make." I broadened my smile, even as my heart pounded. "Surely, an analysis of the income potential was done, and the loan would have been commiserative with that?"

His upper lip lifted, transforming his smile into a sneer. "Why, Misty, I had no idea you held such business acumen."

"While my degree was in counseling, my husband is a politician. You learn a lot about finance when you have to ask for money all the time."

"I'm sure." His white teeth gleamed. "As I said, Ruth is a family friend. We've been very lenient. I assure you I ran the numbers myself and felt quite confident she could make the payments if the cafe had continued at its rate. Sadly, business has declined on the island."

"I suppose it has." I leaned back and crossed my legs. "With North Bridge in such a state of disrepair, it effectively cuts off New Orleans traffic."

"Sadly, yes. And until their Transportation and Development department prioritizes its fix, we have to rely on those willing to make the trek through the wooded area beyond Illusion Square." He mimicked my position, reclining in his seat. "Of course, when I run for mayor, it will be on a platform of improving all the businesses in Treater's Way, from your island cafe to my brother's auto shop."

"Well, if you need tips on effective campaign management, I'm your gal." I cocked finger guns at him, instantly regretting the action. There was no way in hell I was giving this guy campaign tips or more power than he already had. "In the meantime, how do we resolve our problem here?"

He tilted his head as if an idea was forming. "What's your intention for Bridge House, Misty? Do you plan to reopen the Bed and Breakfast portion? Are you staying on Bridge Island?"

I paused. I didn't trust him enough to answer fully. This joker had taken advantage of Ruth. I didn't know what his plan was for the house, but I was certain he'd given her a loan he knew she couldn't pay off.

He wanted the house. I didn't know why, but every fiber of my being told me it was truth. Something was off about this guy, and I was not about to let Ruth be cast out of the only home she'd ever known.

"Yes," I heard myself say. "I will renovate and rebuild Bridge House. I will make it thrive again."

He stared at me until I wanted to fidget, but I held still and set my jaw. I may fall to pieces around put-together women who remind me I'm a hot mess, but this phony was no match for me. Finally, he nodded and grabbed a business card from a marble card holder on the corner of his desk.

"I tell you what." He scribbled on the back of the card. "You have until the end of summer to get Bridge House back to its former glory." He extended the card to me. "This is the name of my go-to contractor. He's done similar jobs, and I happen to know he's available to start right away. Call him. Be sure and tell him I sent you. I will put your loan on hold until the end of August, then we will appraise the new value of the home, and your business plan, Misty, and re-evaluate."

He grazed my finger with his as I took the card. "How does that sound?"

I tucked the card in my back pocket and helped Ruth to stand. I had no idea how I was going to get the money to renovate Bridge House. And for all his pomp and circumstance, it was too easy. Lucas had a plan I didn't understand. Yet.

"Sounds like Aunt Ruth and I are going to have a busy few months." I put my arm around Ruth's shoulder and pulled her away.

I hummed my own tune as we strolled back over South Bridge, sending a wave to Norbert before we turned toward the door. I was awake inside, revitalized and excited, like I hadn't been in years. The more I realized it, the louder the music became.

It was my call, the song of my heart, beautiful and melodic. It could lead me in two directions, toward the water or the house. I had three months to explore them both and figure out which call was stronger.

To do that, I'd have to get to know my mermaid side, to learn how to bring my tail forward.

This was just the beginning.

"You and I belong to each other now." I pressed my hand to the wall, and joy warmed my fingertips as Bridge House welcomed me home.

"But I'm getting rid of that hideous wallpaper."

MISTY MAY NOT HAVE MASTERED the art of being a mermaid, but the work must go on. Bridge House is in dire need of renovation, and it's fighting every decision she makes. What's worse? Her gassy new contractor reeks ... of sabotage.

^^^ Scan the code above or click here to dive into book two: *Bridge Over Stormy Water.*

WHEN A CLUMSY DRAGON turns out to be her scorching hot ex, will an independent therapist reignite an old spark or let it smother?

^^^ Scan the code above or click here to claim your copy of *Not Yet Old Flames* and join my newsletter.

ACKNOWLEDGMENTS

I'd like to thank my amazing mentors at the Writing Wives, Mal and Jill Cooper, for their insight and expertise.

And to my mastermind group, my Jens, your belief in me is beyond anything I might manifest for myself. Thank you for the laughs, tears, data, and joy you bring every day.

ABOUT JB LASSALLE

JB (Jen) Lassalle is a writer of low-steam romantic and urban fantasy. She likes strong females, dimensional males, and found family friendships that triumph over nuanced bad guys you love to hate.

Jen is a New Orleans resident. The city, and the surrounding areas, serve as a rich backdrop for a world where magic exists and mystical creatures are not only real, but live among us.

When Jen isn't writing, she's hanging with her family and friends at a local park or coffee shop. She likes working out, which is kind of weird, loves yoga, and plays video games. Of course, she reads.

Jen and her husband have two kids. One is an avid competitive swimmer (which sucks up all their weekend time). The other is a daydreamer like Jen who plays the Mega Man theme on his guitar and kicks around a soccer ball.

Jen isn't great with social media, but you can connect with her below. Or, join her newsletter when you claim your copy of *Not Yet Old Flames,* a second-chance PWF romantic short.

facebook.com/jblassalle

instagram.com/jblassalle

amazon.com/JB-Lassalle/e/B0BFJXP4GC